Spellbound Ponies

Stacy Gregg (Ngāti Mahuta/Ngāti Pukeko) is the author of Pony Club Secrets, the inspiration for the major TV series MYSTIC.

www.stacygregg.co.uk

Books by Stacy Gregg

The Spellbound Ponies Series

MAGIC AND MISCHIEF
SUGAR AND SPICE
WISHES AND WEDDINGS
FORTUNE AND COOKIES

The Pony Club Secrets series

MYSTIC AND THE MIDNIGHT RIDE
BLAZE AND THE DARK RIDER
DESTINY AND THE WILD HORSES
STARDUST AND THE DAREDEVIL PONIES
COMET AND THE CHAMPION'S CUP
STORM AND THE SILVER BRIDLE
FORTUNE AND THE GOLDEN TROPHY
VICTORY AND THE ALL-STARS ACADEMY
FLAME AND THE REBEL RIDERS
ANGEL AND THE FLYING STALLIONS
LIBERTY AND THE DREAM RIDE
NIGHTSTORM AND THE GRAND SLAM
ISSIE AND THE CHRISTMAS PONY

Pony Club Rival series

THE AUDITIONS
SHOWJUMPERS
RIDING STAR
THE PRIZE

For older readers

THE PRINCESS AND THE FOAL
THE ISLAND OF LOST HORSES
THE GIRL WHO RODE THE WIND
THE DIAMOND HORSE
THE THUNDERBOLT PONY
THE FIRE STALLION
PRINCE OF PONIES
THE FOREVER HORSE

Spellbound Ponies

Fortune and Cookies

STACY GREGG

HarperCollins *Children's Books*

First published in Great Britain by
HarperCollins *Children's Books* in 2021
HarperCollins *Children's Books* is a division of HarperCollins*Publishers* Ltd
HarperCollins Publishers
1 London Bridge Street
London SE1 9GF

www.harpercollins.co.uk

HarperCollins*Publishers*
1st Floor, Watermarque Building, Ringsend Road
Dublin 4, Ireland

1

ISBN 978-0-00-840296-9

A CIP catalogue record for this title is available from the British Library.

Typeset in Cambria Regular 12/24
Printed and bound in the UK using 100% renewable electricity
at CPI Group (UK) Ltd

MIX
Paper from
responsible sources
FSC™ C007454

For Toby and Little Man

Chapter One

Autumn had arrived and the ivy that surrounded the entrance to Pemberley Stables had turned from green to rusty red. Now, as the leaves began to wither and fall, their absence revealed something magical beneath the tangled vines. Words, once hidden, were carved into the stone:

The deepest magic binds these stables
Unless two brave girls can turn the tables.
The curse on each horse must be found,
Then break their spell to be unbound.

As Olivia walked through the stable doors she glanced at the words and remembered when she had first seen them. It had been summer then, and her family had just moved to the village, much to the disgust of her big sister Ella who was furious about leaving London to live in such a 'boring little place'. Olivia, on the other hand, had been thrilled. All she wanted in the world was a pony and with unbelievable luck it had turned out that there were riding stables just up the lane from her new home!

But her hopes had come crashing down when she had arrived at the stables to find them spooky and abandoned. Then, out of nowhere, Eliza had appeared and told Olivia that the stables were spellbound. It had all happened two hundred years ago, when Eliza had suffered a fatal hunting fall from her beloved pony Chessie. Eliza's mother, Lady Luella, in a fit of grief, had paid the Pemberley Witch to cast a spell over all the ponies cursing them for eternity.

'The witch's spell keeps them stuck in time, each one naughty in their own way,' Eliza had explained. 'And I've tried so many times to free them, but I can't do it alone. The spell is quite clear. *Two brave girls* are what's needed!'

As it had turned out, Olivia was very brave indeed. Together with Eliza she had already set three of the ponies free. As she stepped into the stables now, one of those ponies, Bess, stuck her head over the stable door to greet her.

When she had been spellbound, Bess had been a highway horse, a merry thief who loved her life of crime.

'Hello, my beauty.' Olivia stroked the black mare's silken muzzle.

In the stall next to Bess was Prince, who had been rather too fond of cream buns, which had made him too slow to race. And in the stall beside Prince was Sparkle, a stunning white pony who had been a right royal mess until Olivia and Eliza had convinced the mare to smarten up. She'd then been chosen by the Almost-Princess Petronella to ride on her wedding day.

'Looking gorgey-porgey, my sweet Sparkle!' Olivia cooed as she combed out Sparkle's silvery forelock. 'Now, I wonder where Eliza has got to? She was supposed to meet me here to summon another pony but she's nowhere to be—'

'Hi, Livvy!'

'Yikes!' Olivia almost jumped out of her skin as Eliza appeared behind her. 'Stop sneaking up on me like that!' she squeaked.

'Sorry, Livvy!' Eliza giggled. 'That was frightfully ghostly of me. Anyway, I'm so excited that you're here. It's time to break another spell! Are you ready to meet pony number four?'

'Yes, definitely!' Olivia agreed.

The girls stood in front of the fourth stall where the brass name plaque was already beginning to give off a strange glow. In a moment a name would appear on the plaque and then all the girls would need to do was say the name out loud as they stepped over the threshold, and a new Spellbound pony would appear.

'I can see the letters starting to form . . .' Eliza whispered.

'Oh yes! Any minute now . . .' Olivia agreed.

Olivia and Eliza were so busy staring at the plaque that they didn't notice a ghostly mist rising up behind them. It oozed through the corridor until it completely covered the floor. Suddenly, with a mysterious swoosh, the stable doors opened all by themselves and a dark figure hovered into view. She was cloaked in black velvet, her skin as pale as a statue, her lips scarlet red and her eyebrows arched imperiously. Silently she floated across the mist through the gloom until she was right behind Olivia and Eliza.

'Hello, girls!'

'Eek!' Olivia and Eliza both leaped in surprise.

'Oh, Mama!' Eliza said, clutching at her heart. 'Goodness. You scared me to death!'

'You can't be scared to death, Eliza – you're already a ghost!' Olivia pointed out.

'Well, it gave me a fright at any rate,' Eliza huffed. 'It's very rude sneaking up on someone like that!'

'Yes, exactly!' Olivia agreed. 'That's precisely how I feel when you sneak up on me, Eliza!'

Eliza sniffed. 'Really, Livvy, you complain a lot, but I do think these things are to be expected when your best friend is a ghost!'

'Ahem,' Lady Luella interrupted, 'perhaps you girls might have this conversation about the rights and wrongs of sneaking up another time and instead we could talk about why *I'm* here?'

'Yes, good idea, Mama,' Eliza said, looking relieved to be off the hook.

'Have you come to help us to break the spell?' Olivia asked hopefully.

Lady Luella looked at the glowing plaque. 'You know I cannot do that, child. It's true I was the one who paid the witch to create the curse but I have no powers over her magic. Witches' spells are tricky things – and there's more to this one than you think.'

'Then why have you come, Mama?' Eliza wanted to know.

'I am here on a matter of great importance . . .' Lady Luella said. Her expression was so grave that Olivia felt her heart pounding as she watched Lady Luella reach beneath her black-velvet riding coat and pull out a white envelope that she handed to Eliza.

'Contained inside is all you need to know,' she said. 'Farewell, Eliza, dear heart. Until we meet again.'

Lady Luella waved them farewell and floated out just as she had arrived, on a cloud of enchanted mist, leaving Eliza holding the envelope.

'Eliza, come on, open it!' Olivia said.

Eliza, looking worried, took a deep breath, opened the envelope and pulled out a golden card.

'Ooh!' she squeaked.

'What is it?' Olivia asked nervously.

'You'll never believe it, Livvy,' Eliza said. 'We've been invited to a party!'

Eliza and Olivia

Chapter Two

Lady Luella of Pemberley Manor
requests the company of her daughter,
Eliza, and best friend, Olivia, for the
200th-year celebration fête. To be held on
the manor lawn next Saturday at noon.

'What's a fête exactly?' said Olivia.

'It's like a big garden party and the whole village comes along,' Eliza explained. 'There are wonderful stalls selling treats of all kinds and animals on parade and lots of games—'

'Games? What kind of games?'

'Oh, the usual thing,' Eliza said. 'Guess the weight of the bull, duck racing, black pudding hurling—'

'Duck racing? Wouldn't the jockeys have to be very, very small?'

Eliza laughed. 'Oh, now you're just being silly! No one rides them! But you can make a bundle betting on which of the ducks is the fastest. There'll be jugglers too, I imagine, and fire-eaters, and there's always a fortune-teller, and did I mention there's lots of scrummy food? Hot roasted chestnuts and sweet mince cakes . . .'

'It sounds like you want to go,' Olivia said.

'I suppose I do,' Eliza agreed. 'It's been two hundred years since the last one and I have so missed all the fun of the fair. There's always a big showjumping contest at the end. I actually won it myself once. I rode our Pemberley Golden Boy, Champ, Mama's boldest and most brilliant jumping pony, and we got a clear round even though the fences were frightfully huge!'

'Why do you think Lady Luella is holding the fête again after all this time?' Olivia was suspicious. 'You know she's always trying to get you to return home to live with her in the manor, Eliza.'

'Oh, she must know by now that I'll never leave Spellbound Stables until all the ponies are free,' Eliza said breezily. 'No, I expect it's just that she couldn't let the two hundredth anniversary go by without a celebration. Come on, Livvy, we should go. Did I mention there's lots of scrummy food?'

'I do like scrummy food . . .' Olivia admitted.

All this time, as the girls had been talking, the plaque on the stable door had been glowing more and more brightly, and now it shone and twinkled like a star.

Olivia gasped. 'Look! Do you see that? The name has appeared! It's time to summon a new pony!'

Eliza clapped her hands with glee. 'Time to cross the threshold!'

She stood beside Olivia and the two girls stepped into the stall and called out the name on the door. '*Champ!*'

'Ooh, it's Mama's showjumper!' said Eliza.

Once again a ghostly mist rose from the straw on the floor and soon it filled the stall.

'I can't see a thing!' Olivia said. 'Eliza? Where are you?'

'I'm right here!' said Eliza.

'Me too!' another voice said. 'I'm here as well. In fact, I think I was here first and I was definitely here the best!'

And then the mist cleared and standing in the middle of the stall with a brilliant red winner's sash round his glossy neck was a handsome palomino pony.

'Champ's the name,' the pony said brightly, 'and winning's the game!'

'So this is our new Spellbound pony?' Olivia said. 'I wonder what's wrong with him.'

Champ gave a chortle. 'Wrong with me? You're in need of a check-up from the neck up asking a question like that! Nothing is wrong with me. Nothing at all! I'm the perfect pony.'

'Hmmm,' Olivia said. 'The thing is, Champ, I'm not trying to be mean, but you've been spellbound by the Pemberley Witch. She's cursed you in some way, so we need to find out what your problem is so that we can help you.'

Champ's chortle now became a guffaw as he lay down on the straw and rolled about in amusement, kicking his legs up in the air.

'Ha ha ha! Hee-hee-hee!' he laughed. 'I'm too clever for the witch. In fact, I'm the only pony in the stables who has ever outwitted her.'

'Really?' Olivia was surprised. 'It's just that if you aren't spellbound, then shouldn't you be a real-life pony again? Not a talking one like you are right now?'

'Oh, that'll happen soon enough,' Champ reassured her. 'Why, I was just saying to the prime minister the other day over lunch at his country estate—'

'Wait!' Olivia stopped him. 'You had lunch with the prime minister?'

Champ snorted. 'Of course I did! He wanted to congratulate me on my recent space mission. Did you know I was the first pony on the moon?'

'Crikey!' Eliza said. 'The first pony on the moon! Isn't modern science amazing? I could never have imagined such a thing two hundred and nine years ago when I was born.'

'What's it like up there on the moon then?' Olivia asked suspiciously.

'It's a bit dull,' Champ said. 'You know, not much atmosphere! Ha ha!'

Olivia groaned. 'Very funny.'

'Of course as soon as I came back down to Earth I went to Ascot and I won all the races,' Champ continued, 'and the queen came to watch and gave me a special medal for being the best at everything. And then afterwards she took me out to dinner to say thank you.'

'And why was she thanking you?' Olivia asked suspiciously.

'Well, because I had done something super-amazing, as always,' Champ replied, flicking his flaxen mane. 'I'd just invented Christmas, you see, and she said I deserved an extra treat for being so brilliant.'

'You . . . invented Christmas?' Olivia was gobsmacked.

'Wowsers!' Eliza said. 'I imagine she did want to thank you. We all love Christmas!'

'You're welcome!' Champ said.

Olivia rolled her eyes. 'I think we've heard enough, thanks, Champ. Eliza and I need to go outside and talk for a bit.'

'Take as long as you need,' Champ called after them as they closed the stall behind them. 'I'll just be in here being brilliant as usual!'

'Phew!' Olivia exclaimed once they were safely out of Champ's earshot. 'Well, we've got our work cut out for us this time!'

'I know!' Eliza agreed. 'He does seem perfect, doesn't he? How will we possibly find out what is wrong with him?'

Olivia boggled. 'Are you being daft on purpose, Eliza? It's obvious what's wrong with Champ!'

'It is?' Eliza frowned. 'I think he's rather an

impressive pony, Livvy. Winner of Ascot! First pony on the moon! Lunch with the prime minister! Dinner with the queen!'

Olivia groaned. 'Don't you see? None of it is true! Champ is a big fat fibber.'

'Oh.' Eliza went quiet for a moment. 'Now that you say it, that does make more sense.'

'Yes,' Olivia agreed. 'Champ is telling porkies. He's been cursed to tell utter whoppers, and if we're going to save him, then we have to make him stop lying and start telling the truth.'

'Oh, absolutely!' Eliza agreed. 'Except, I wonder . . .' She hesitated.

'Yes?' Olivia said. 'Tell me. What did you wonder exactly?'

'Was all of it a lie really, Livvy? Or did he actually invent Christmas?'

Olivia sighed a long, deep, despairing sigh. Eliza

would grasp the truth eventually, but there was one thing Olivia already knew to be true: Champ was going to be their toughest Spellbound pony yet!

Chapter Three

The next morning, when Olivia arrived at the stables, she found Eliza watching, enthralled, as Champ placed a block of wood on top of some bricks in the middle of the stall.

'Livvy! You're just in time!' Eliza said. 'Did you know that Champ is a black belt in karate? He's about to judo-chop this wood in half for us!'

Olivia looked at Champ in disbelief. 'You're a

black belt? How on earth would a pony ever learn karate?'

Champ chortled. 'Oh, Livvy! There are some things I can't reveal - I took an oath, you see, when I was a secret agent working for the government.'

'You were a secret agent?' Eliza squeaked. 'How daring!'

'Oh yes.' Champ nodded. 'It was a life of danger, all right, being a spy. When the government sent me undercover to Russia to steal back a nuclear weapon, the freedom of the whole world depended on me.'

'Oh, good grief,' Olivia groaned. She looked at Eliza, hoping that her friend could see that Champ was lying, but Eliza seemed to be lapping it up.

'So anyway,' Champ continued, 'I took an oath not to share the secrets that I uncovered. So I can't really talk about it, girls - for your own safety, you see. You'd be in danger if you knew too much.'

Olivia rolled her eyes. 'Champ, you really need to stop this nonsense. I know you're telling fibs.'

'Am I?' Champ laughed. 'Or are you working for the Russians?'

'Of course I'm not working for the Russians!' Olivia lost her temper. 'Champ. You're a big fat fibber and it needs to stop or the witch's curse will never be broken and you'll stay spellbound forever.'

'I know!' Eliza said brightly. 'Champ – if you really are a top-secret spy and a black belt in karate, then you can prove it to Livvy by breaking the wood in half!'

Olivia smiled and folded her arms. 'Yes, Champ. Why don't you prove it? Chop the block in half and I'll admit that you are a karate master.'

Champ looked nervous. 'Uhhhh . . . I could chop the block of wood; of course I could. My hooves are registered as lethal weapons . . .'

'Here it comes . . .' Olivia muttered to Eliza.

'Watch him weasel out of it.'

'And I would do it for you right now,' Champ continued, 'except it's the strangest thing. I ran a marathon this morning and I won the gold medal, but as I was crossing the finishing line I think I sprained my fetlock. So I went to see the doctor and he said I was absolutely forbidden from chopping blocks of wood for at least a week.'

'How convenient!' Olivia scoffed.

'Well, it's not really convenient at all,' Champ insisted, 'not for an all-round champion superstar athlete like me. Still, hopefully I'll be given a clean bill of health by the doc soon and I can chop wood to my heart's content. Until then, I might just take up skydiving again . . .'

'Oh, I give up!' Olivia stomped out of Champ's stall and had reached the stable entrance when Eliza caught up with her.

'Livvy, don't go!' she said. 'Please stay and help save Champ!'

Olivia turned round with her hands on her hips. 'And listen to all that rot he's spouting?'

'He's not a bad pony, truly he's not,' Eliza said. 'It's the witch's curse that's making him tell lies. We have to help him and return him to the stables.'

'But how?' Olivia groaned. 'Every time I try, he just keeps telling bigger and bigger lies!'

Eliza looked like she was going to cry. 'I don't know, but we have to save him, Livvy. It's so very sad. If Champ can't be de-spelled, then he'll never be free and happy like Bess and Prince and Sparkle. Look at them! They're so delighted to be real-life ponies again.'

Olivia looked out across the green pasture beside the stables to where the three ponies were merrily cantering. 'They are happy, aren't they?' she agreed.

'They certainly are,' Eliza said. 'Although I've been meaning to say that now autumn is upon us it's getting rather chilly and all three of them could do with warm stable rugs.'

'I saw some very nice woolly ones at the tack store in town,' Olivia said, 'but they were quite expensive and we've already spent most of our money on hay. How could we possibly afford rugs?'

'Oooh! I know!' Eliza looked like a bulb had just pinged above her head. 'We could set up our own stall at the fête! Lots of people do it! They sell all kinds of things – jams and chutneys, oh, and cakes! You know how to bake, don't you, Livvy?'

'I suppose I do now, yes,' Olivia said, thinking about how her baking efforts had helped to de-spell Prince. 'I have a cookie recipe at home I've been meaning to try.'

'Perfect!' Eliza clapped her hands in delight. 'You bake a huge stack of cookies and we'll make pots of money and have more than enough to buy autumn rugs for the ponies.'

'And what about saving Champ?' Olivia asked.

'We shall have to keep thinking about that,' Eliza said. 'But promise me you won't give up.'

Olivia smiled. 'Of course not.'

Eliza beamed. 'Oh, hooray! *Two brave girls together*; I know we can do it.'

The girls were so busy watching the ponies at play that they failed to notice the rotund figure of Horace the Hunt Master as he slunk through the stable door lugging an enormous sack.

Horace was Lady Luella's sidekick and he was always playing tricks on them. As he bounded down the corridor with his bundle slung across his back, his bouncing strides made his neck wobble about like mad. It never did sit still on his shoulders as a consequence of having been broken two hundred years ago in the fateful hunting accident when Eliza and her pony, Chessie, had got in his way. Horace had never forgiven Eliza for that dreadful day and he liked to pay her back by causing mischief at the stables.

'Greetings, my dear Champ!' Horace stuck his head into the Spellbound pony's stall. 'I hear you are quite the yarn-spinner, a fantastic fabricator of fiction!'

'I'm a what?' Champ said.

'I'm saying you're a liar, my boy.' Horace chortled. 'And a rather good one to boot.' Horace rubbed his hands together with glee. 'Champ, my champion, you're just the kind of teller of tales I've been looking to make mischief with.'

'I am?' Champ said. 'Hey, what have you got in that sack?'

'That's for me to know,' Horace gloated, 'and for you to find out. Just as soon as you agree to come and work for me.'

'Okay, I'm in!' Champ said. 'So what's the job?'

Horace reached into his sack and pulled out a turban covered in golden stars and a snowglobe filled with golden flakes.

'Champ, my fortunate fibbing friend –' Horace beamed – 'we've got a date with the Pemberley Manor Fête.'

Chapter Four

Olivia opened the cookbook and it fell open on the page for ginger cookies.

Oh, super-scrummy! She hummed merrily to herself as she read through the list of ingredients and set about ferreting them out of the cupboards. *Our cookies are going to be the hit of the fête, and those ponies will be wearing cosy new autumn rugs in no time!*

She looked at the clock. *Yikes! How did it get to be so late?* It was already eleven and she had promised Eliza she'd be at the stables by midday!

Hurrying, Olivia began to throw the ingredients into the mixing bowl as fast as she could. Two cups of flour. Five tablespoons of cream. A cup of melted butter . . .

The batter wobbled in a weird way as she spooned it on to the baking tray.

That's a bit odd, Olivia thought. Even odder, once they were in the oven the cookies oozed out like flat little rocks.

I'll just take another look at the recipe book, Olivia thought. And that was when she discovered her mistake.

Olivia groaned. 'I missed out half the ingredients because the pages were stuck together!' she said out loud.

'Oh, that was me!' Olivia's sister, Ella, confessed breezily as she walked in. 'I got the book covered in sticky syrup the other day.'

'Do you think it really matters if I missed out the baking powder?' Olivia asked her mum. 'And the ginger?'

'Well,' Mrs Campbell said kindly, 'baking powder

is what makes them light and fluffy, so that would

have been nice. And I suppose the ginger would have

been good too, since they are ginger cookies.'

Ella snatched up a cookie from the cooling rack.

'Don't!' Olivia said. 'I need them all.'

'You won't miss *one*, Livvy! I just want a taste!'

Ella taunted. She took a bite but promptly spat it out

again. 'Ick! They're sour!'

'Oh, yes.' Olivia sighed. 'I didn't put any sugar in them either!'

'Never mind,' said Mrs Campbell, smiling. 'You can start again and make a fresh batch.'

Olivia shoved the cookies in a tin and ran for the door. 'I can't,' she said. 'I'm utterly out of time!'

As it was, the clock had struck twelve when she finally arrived at Pemberley Stables and Eliza was in a tizz!

'Oh, Livvy! Champ is missing!' her friend said, fretting. 'I just went to check his stall and saw this note on his door. It says he had to leave immediately to take charge of a teacup factory in Outer Mongolia.'

'Yes,' Olivia said, 'well, I think we can safely assume that's a lie. Anyway, we don't have time to worry about Champ right now; we need to get to the fête.'

She passed Eliza her backpack. 'Here, I brought you some clothes to wear.'

'Oh, thank you!' Eliza was delighted as she pulled on jeans and a T-shirt. 'A flouncy nightie is all well and good when you are wafting around a ghostly stables, but jeans are much more practical for a country fête. Right then! Off we go!'

As she said this, a ghostly mist began creeping up through the straw on the floor of Champ's stall. Soon the mist covered the girls' feet, and then their shins, and very quickly it filled the stall so Olivia couldn't see a thing.

A moment later the mist cleared and they were no longer inside the stall. They were outdoors on the lawn in front of Pemberley Manor, the grand stately home where Eliza had grown up.

'Wowsers!' Olivia had never seen the manor like this before. 'It's like a fairground!'

Eliza clapped her hands in delight. 'The fête has begun! Oh, it's every bit as much fun as I remember! Look! There are duck races over there! And that's the bull – you have to guess how much he weighs!

And how adorable are the pink prize pigs? Oooh, and snowy-white sheep with black faces! And look, Livvy, this must be our stall! Let's set up our wares!

'It looks very pretty!' Olivia said, admiring the cheerful red-and-white bunting and the red-and-white-checked tablecloth.

'I'll put the cookies out in the baskets,' Eliza suggested. 'You do the blackboard!'

Olivia took a piece of chalk and wrote:

OLIVIA AND ELIZA'S SUPER-YUMMY, DELICIOUS SWEET GINGER COOKIES. ONE GOLD COIN EACH

'What do you think?' Olivia said.

'They sound marvellous,' Eliza said. 'I'm sure people will snap them up and we'll be sold out in no time. Oh, look, Livvy! Here comes a customer! It's the Duchess of Derryshire!' she squealed.

'Two cookies for my daughters, please!' the duchess said.

'Here you are, madam,' Olivia said, handing the cookies over with a nervous smile.

But when the girls bit into them they both burst
into tears.

'They taste yucky!' the girls cried.

'I demand a refund!' the duchess fumed.

Eliza sighed as she watched the angry duchess stomp off. 'This is not going well at all.'

'I know,' Olivia agreed. 'I wish we were like that tent over there! Everyone is buzzing round it like bees round a honeypot. I wonder what's inside?'

'Let's ask someone!' Eliza replied brightly.

At that very moment the bishop walked past, whistling merrily and clutching a candyfloss stick in one hand and his prize racing duck in the other.

'I say, bishop!' Eliza called out. 'What's happening in that purple tent over there? The one covered with golden moons and stars.'

'It's the fortune-teller,' the bishop said, rolling his eyes.

'The chap in the tent tells your future. Apparently he's been coming up with the most preposterous nonsense and everyone is lapping it up.'

'Is that so?' Olivia's suspicions were aroused. 'What's the name of this fortune-teller?'

'He calls himself the Great Palomino,' the bishop said with a sigh. 'Honestly, people will believe all sorts of mystical poppycock given half the chance. Anyway, I can't stop and chat, I'd better get back to my church and prepare the sermon.'

'Do you want to buy a cookie before you go?' Eliza asked hopefully.

'No thanks,' the bishop replied. 'I've heard about your cookies from the Duchess of Derryshire and I think it would be safer to give them a miss.'

'Well, that is a worry,' Eliza said as they watched him go. 'It appears our cookies now have a bad reputation.'

'Never mind that!' Olivia said. 'We need to get over to that tent immediately!'

'Why?' Eliza said. 'Oh! Do you think perhaps the fortune-teller can help us to find Champ?'

Olivia sighed. 'Yes, Eliza. I do. I think it's time we paid a visit to the Great Palomino.'

Chapter Five

Olivia marched straight up to the fortune-teller's tent and was about to lift the purple-velvet curtain and step inside when she felt a hand grasp her firmly by the shoulder.

'Excuse me!' A rather cross-looking woman in a very bold feathered hat harrumphed at her. 'There's a queue here, you know. I've been waiting for almost an hour now, so don't think you can jump in! Get to the back!'

Olivia looked behind her to see that there was indeed a queue and it snaked halfway round the fête. 'Oh no,' she said to the woman. 'You see, I'm not trying to jump the queue. I just want to talk to the fortune-teller.'

'Precisely my point!' the woman scoffed. 'We all want to talk to the fortune-teller! Join the queue!'

'What shall we do?' Olivia hissed at Eliza. 'She won't let me in!'

'I don't think we have any choice,' Eliza replied.

And so the girls walked all the way to the end of the queue and waited. And waited.

'Can you see anything?' Olivia wanted to know.

'I can see them going into the velvet tent one at a time, and then they spend ages in there.' Eliza sighed. 'I wonder what the Great Palomino is telling them?'

'Oh, he says the most marvellous things!' trilled a young dairy maid who was now in the queue behind them. 'My big sister told me I absolutely had to come and see him! She had a session with the fortune-teller this morning and he told her she would become a world-famous ballerina.'

'Oh?' Olivia said. 'Is your sister a good dancer?'

'Not really, now you mention it,' the dairy maid admitted. 'She's a bit of a clod-foot actually. Father always said she was so clumsy she could trip over a pattern in the carpet. Still, if the fortune-teller says it, surely it's bound to come true?'

'Oh! Yes!' a woman further back in the queue piped up. 'It's only a matter of time before the Great Palomino's mystic pronouncements bear fruit. Why, just this morning he told my aunt she would learn to play the bagpipes like an angel and open her own cheese store.'

'And let me guess –' Olivia rolled her eyes – 'she's never played the bagpipes before?'

'Never!' the old woman replied. 'And she hates cheese! Allergic, in fact! Yet there you go! She's off to buy a set of bagpipes now and churn some Cheddar. That's fate for you.'

Olivia sighed. 'Isn't it, just?'

And so it went on. It seemed like everyone in the queue had an exciting story to share about the fortune-teller's predictions for someone they knew. And slowly, slowly the queue ahead grew smaller until at last Olivia and Eliza were at the entrance to the velvet tent.

Eliza peered inside. 'Oooh, it's very dark in there. I wonder . . .'

'Welcome, welcome . . .' a spooky voice said from inside the tent. 'Step inside and discover your destiny . . .'

'Hey!' Olivia said. 'That voice sounds awfully familiar.'

'The Great Palomino will tell your fortune in just a moment,' the voice continued, 'but first you must put five gold coins into the pot.'

'Five gold coins!' Eliza breathed. 'Gosh, that is a lot of money!'

'Not really,' the spooky voice replied. 'It's quite a reasonable amount to find out what the future has in store.'

'Hmmm, I suppose that's true,' Eliza said. And Olivia, seeing they had no choice in the matter, dug into her purse and dropped five coins into the pot.

'I've paid!' she called out into the gloom of the tent.

'Excellent, excellent,' the spooky voice said. 'And now you may find out your fate. It is time for you to meet . . . the Great Palomino!'

Suddenly the purple curtains parted to reveal a table with a crystal ball on it and a stack of tarot cards. Sitting behind the table was the Great Palomino himself, dressed in a velvet cloak and a turban covered in sparkly stars and moons.

'The Great Palomino welcomes you! Please take a seat . . .' the fortune-teller began to say, and then he gave a startled squeak. 'Oh no! It's Eliza and Olivia!'

'Oh, I say!' Eliza gasped. 'What a clever fortune-teller he is! Look, Olivia! He knew our names right away! Oh, mystical fortune-teller – your powers are indeed great! Please tell us what the future holds?'

'Well,' the fortune-teller replied, 'I foresee that in a moment Olivia here is going to get angry.'

'Angry? I'm furious!' Olivia fumed.

'Oh, goodness,' Eliza said. 'He's right again! It's all coming true!'

'Eliza!' Olivia sighed. 'Stop it! Have you not figured out who the Great Palomino is yet?' She reached out and yanked away the fortune-teller's turban and cloak to reveal . . .

Eliza was stunned. 'Champ!'

'Of course it's Champ!' Olivia said. 'He's had the whole village sucked in with his ridiculous lies!'

'Oh, don't be so grumpy, Livvy!' Champ swished his tail merrily. 'I've been having fun making up all kinds of nonsense. And these people just lap it all up! I'm a total natural!'

'He certainly is,' the spooky voice piped up, and now Horace the Hunt Master revealed himself. He was holding tightly on to a large pot filled to the brim with gold coins.

'Good work, Champ, my boy,' he announced. 'I've made a pile of loot, so I'll be on my way.' And with his head bobbling about like mad, the hunt master made a mad dash out of the tent and was gone.

Olivia turned on Champ. 'I can't believe you let that dreadful Horace trick you into telling lies and taking gold from all those poor people!'

'Oh, don't be silly, Livvy!' Champ scoffed. 'They loved it! Besides, telling lies never hurt anyone . . .'

But at that moment the most terrible commotion could be heard outside the tent, and then the old woman they'd met in the queue stuck her head inside.

'Help, help!' she shouted. 'Oh, please come quickly!'

'Why? What on earth has happened?' Olivia said.

'It's my aunt!' the old woman cried. 'She blew too hard and exploded her bagpipes. And now the doctors are racing her to hospital.'

'Because of the exploding bagpipes?' Eliza asked.

'No!' the old woman cried. 'She'd managed to recover from that and had returned to her cheese churn when she thought she'd better taste a piece and of course she's terribly allergic and now her whole face has puffed up like a round of brie.'

'Well, well,' Champ said, 'I didn't see that coming!'

'But that's the whole point! You're *supposed* to predict the future!' the woman bawled.

'I can predict one thing for sure,' Olivia said, 'this whole fortune-telling caper has gone horribly wrong.'

Eliza peeked outside. 'You're right about that!' she squeaked. 'There's an angry mob out there and they're coming this way! What are we going to do?'

Olivia thought fast. 'Don't worry,' she said. 'I have

a plan that will save the fête and you too, Champ. But to make it work we need to get back to the cookie stall!'

'Not a problem,' Champ said, 'the Great Palomino knows a secret exit! Jump aboard, girls!'

And with a swish of the velvet curtains, just like magic mist, they were gone.

Chapter Six

It was just in time! As the angry mob carrying pitchforks and torches stormed the front of the tent, Champ, with the girls astride him, snuck out the back.

'I don't understand why they're cross,' Champ snorted as they galloped away. 'They asked me to tell their fortunes!'

'But the things you said weren't true, Champ!' Olivia sighed. 'This is what we've been trying to tell you! Lies always catch up with you and get you into trouble in the end.'

'Yes, it's got to stop, Champ,' Eliza agreed. 'I know you've been cursed, but can't you try to tell the truth?'

Champ looked downhearted. 'Oh, girls, I don't even know how to be truthful! It's been so long.'

'Don't worry,' Olivia said, 'we're going to help you. Quick! To the cookie stall!'

At the stall Olivia leaped off Champ's back and went hunting under the tablecloth. 'Aha!' she said. 'I thought I saw these earlier!'

She emerged with some pretty scraps of paper and a ball of twisty red-and-white string.

'What's all this for?' Champ asked. 'Are we wrapping presents?'

'No. We're going to make fortune cookies,' Olivia said.

'Hasn't fortune-telling already got Champ into enough trouble?' Eliza asked.

'Aaah,' Olivia said, 'but these fortune cookies will be different!'

Olivia grabbed the blackboard from the front of the stall and wiped away the words OLIVIA AND ELIZA'S SUPER-YUMMY, DELICIOUS SWEET GINGER COOKIES. And instead she wrote:

THE HONEST BAKER'S
SUGAR-FREE TRUTHFUL
FORTUNE COOKIES!

'Champ,' Olivia said, 'your job is to write the fortunes on these pieces of paper for each cookie. No fibs this time, though – nothing but the truth!'

After each fortune was done Olivia used the

red-and-white string to wrap the paper round the cookies and put them back in the basket.

'Oh, I hope this works!' Eliza said.

'Me too!' Olivia agreed. She looked at Champ who had the pen grasped in his teeth and was scribbling furiously. 'Can you write any faster, Champ? The angry mob have seen us and are coming this way!'

The mob looked very cross as they stomped

through the fête. Leading them was the dairy maid, pitchfork in hand. Beside her was a young girl hobbling on crutches.

'Oh, hello!' Olivia tried to be cheerful. 'Everything okay?'

'Okay?' the dairy maid scoffed. 'Does it look like things are okay?' She gestured to the girl beside her on crutches. 'This is my sister. The Great Palomino

told her to become a ballerina and she immediately twisted her ankle trying to dance *Swan Lake*!'

'I tripped over a pattern in the carpet!' the ballerina explained. 'This is all your fault, Great Palomino!'

'Yes, Great Palomino,' the angry mob chorused, 'you've got a lot of explaining to do!'

'Wait!' Olivia cried. 'I know you're all upset but it's not Champ's fault. He's been under a dreadful witch's curse that makes him fib and now he's changed his ways. Look! He's made fortune cookies for you all to say sorry!'

'Cookies, you say?' The dairy maid put her pitchfork down. 'I do love cookies!'

'And these are super-special honest fortune cookies,' Olivia pointed out. 'Give her one, Champ!'

Champ handed a cookie to the dairy maid who unwrapped it and read it out loud. 'It says, "Stop listening to your sister. Get a mind of your own!"'

The ballerina took a cookie too and unwrapped the paper. 'Mine says, "You have two left feet and should give up dancing entirely!"'

Olivia boggled at Champ.

Champ shrugged. 'What? You told me to be honest!'

'You could have been a bit nicer, though!' she said.

'Oh, not at all!' the ballerina said. 'Truly it's the first time anyone has been forthright about my lack of talent. I mean, it's such dreadfully hard work being a ballerina, all that tiptoeing and leaping about for hours on end. Now I can give it up with a clear conscience, and once my ankle has healed I can pursue my real dream of becoming a vet!'

'Yes,' the dairy maid said, 'I agree with my sister. How wonderful to be told the truth for once! It gives you such a fresh perspective—'

'Excuse me! I hate to interrupt but there's a big queue and we'd all like some service, please!'

It was the Duchess of Derryshire. 'A cookie, please!' the duchess trilled.

'Are you sure, duchess?' Olivia asked nervously. 'Last time you demanded a refund?'

'Oh, but these are sugar-free cookies!' the duchess said, pointing at the blackboard. 'How marvellously healthy! Very fashionable!'

'They do taste a bit like cardboard, though,' Champ warned her.

'How very honest of you to tell me that!' The duchess smiled at him. 'Make it a dozen!'

Olivia was impressed. 'Yes, Champ. I think you're really getting the hang of this honesty thing!'

'These honest sugar-free cookies are going like hot cakes!' Eliza said. 'They're a real hit!'

It was true. The angry mob were now a happy mob as they opened up their fortunes and read them and fell about laughing or found themselves nodding in agreement with Champ's messages.

'Interesting,' Champ observed. 'I thought my fibs made me popular, but now I see that telling the truth is a much better way to make friends.'

'The cookies are all gone!' Eliza said brightly as she handed over the last one.

'Have we made enough money to buy rugs for the ponies?' Olivia asked.

'Oh, that's a good point,' Eliza said. 'I didn't actually charge for them.'

Olivia sighed. 'I suppose that's fair enough since Horace stole that gold from everyone in the first place. But how will we make enough money to get the rugs? The poor things will freeze to death without them.'

'Frozen ponies!' Champ whinnied. 'How terrible! And all because of me and my lies?'

'You mustn't blame yourself, Champ,' Olivia said kindly. 'It was the witch's curse that made you do it.'

'Oh, but I do blame myself!' Champ said. 'And I'm going to fix it. I'm going to make us a fortune and save the ponies. Leave it to me!'

'Champ? What are you going to do?' Olivia asked.

'You'll see!' Champ said. And with a dramatic

swish of his tail he reared up on his hind legs, turned and bolted away.

'Goodness!' Eliza exclaimed. 'What in heaven's name do you think Champ has in mind this time?'

'I don't know,' Olivia groaned, 'but it's bound to be trouble!'

Chapter Seven

The girls searched the entire fête but there was no sign of Champ.

'There's a commotion over there,' Olivia said, pointing beyond the fire-eaters, the black pudding tossers and the Ferris wheel. 'Let's go!'

When they reached the marquee they could see lots of colourful fences all arranged in the field.

'Oh, they've set up for the showjumping,' Eliza said.

'It must be about to begin.'

'Look at the size of those jumps!' Olivia squeaked. 'They're enormous!'

'Nonsense, Livvy,' came a familiar voice from behind the marquee. 'Those fences will be easy-peasy-pudding for a champion showjumper like me!'

Olivia turned round to see Champ. He was wearing a rather serious-looking saddle and bridle.

'Champ! Why are you dressed like that! And where on earth did you get to?'

'Yes, sorry to bolt off like that,' Champ said, 'but I needed to get changed and scoot to the judges' tent to make a last-minute entry into the showjumping.'

Olivia boggled. 'You mean you've entered?'

'Oh, don't worry, I put your name down too, Livvy!' Champ said brightly. 'You're going to be riding me!'

'That's ridiculous!' Olivia said. 'I've never showjumped in my life.'

'Aaah, but I have,' Champ said. 'At least somewhere in my memory I get the sneaking feeling that I once was a showjumper. And what's more – I'm pretty sure I was amazing at it too!'

'Champ!' Olivia was furious. 'You big, boastful fibber! Are you telling lies again?'

'Oh, Livvy, not at all!' Champ laughed. 'Truly I'm a showjumping superstar. I'll fly over those fences with springs in my hooves and we'll take home the prize money and buy rugs for the ponies.'

'Uhh, Livvy?' Eliza interrupted. 'This time he's actually telling the truth.'

She turned to look at Champ with wide green eyes. 'Champ, think hard now and cast your mind back two hundred years to the last Pemberley Manor Fête. Do you remember it?'

'Why, yes!' Champ said. 'Strangely enough, now that you mention it, I do!'

♥ 80 ♥

'Me too!' Eliza said, smiling. 'I was there with you. That was the day I competed with you in the showjumping . . . my Pemberley Golden Boy!'

Champ's ears pricked forward. *Pemberley Golden Boy? Eliza! I recall how you always called me by that name! Oh, I'm remembering it all now! You were the one who rode me to victory!*

'Wait!' Olivia was stunned. 'So Champ really is a superstar jumper? He's not fibbing this time?'

'He's not fibbing this time,' Eliza confirmed.

Told you so, Champ said with satisfaction.

'Well, if you rode him to glory once before,' Olivia said, 'then surely, Eliza, you should be the one who rides him again?'

'Oh, but I can't, Livvy!' Eliza reached out a hand and her fingers slipped straight through Champ's golden mane as if they were made of mist. 'I'm a ghost,' Eliza reminded her. 'You'll have to do it.'

'I can't possibly! The jumps are too scary!' Olivia squeaked. 'Look! That water jump is as wide as a car! The brick wall is seven feet tall and that triple combination is higher than my head!'

'Hang on a minute . . .' Champ said. 'Oooh, I'm remembering something else now. It's this old poem I know. Don't ask me why but for some reason I feel it might be important . . .'

And the words he spoke next sent a chill down Olivia's spine.

'The deepest magic binds these stables
Unless two brave girls can turn the tables.
The curse on each horse must be found,
Then break their spell to be unbound.'

'That's not a poem!' Eliza said. 'It's the curse of Spellbound Stables! Oh, Champ, you're a genius! Of course. The showjumping must be the key! *Two brave girls can turn the tables*! The first girl was me when I won it. And now it's your turn, Livvy! You must have to ride a clear round on Champ to break the curse?'

'Eek! Do you think?' Olivia looked at the

enormous jumps. 'There's absolutely no other way?

'I'm afraid not,' Eliza said. 'If we're going to save the Spellbound ponies, it's up to you, Livvy. This is your moment of truth. Are you brave enough?'

Chapter Eight

Round the arena an excited crowd had gathered to watch the showjumping.

'Hasn't it been terribly thrilling so far?' the dairy maid enthused.

'Yes! The jumps are so huge that no one has managed a clear round yet!' the former ballerina agreed.

'And now the very last rider and pony are

entering the arena,' the Duchess of Derryshire said. 'Oh, look! What a gorgeous palomino! And doesn't he look familiar?'

'Very familiar,' the dairy maid said.

'Why, isn't that the Great Palomino himself?' the ballerina exclaimed.

'Yes!' the dairy maid said. 'It's Champ! Yay, Champ!'

It was indeed Champ, and on his back, looking completely terrified and holding on for dear life, was Olivia.

'Countdown to take-off, Livvy,' Champ said as he circled the jumps, eyeing the big brick wall for size.

'I can't believe I'm doing this!' Olivia squeaked. 'Is it too late to withdraw?'

Champ snorted. 'Afraid so! There's the bell! Time to fly, Livvy! Hey-ho, let's go! Three, two, one, and we're off!'

With a swish of his silvery tail and a flash of his hooves Champ flew in boldly at the first jump.

'Oooooh noooo!' Olivia shut her eyes and held her breath as Champ charged down on the wall. When she opened her eyes to take a peek she gave an *eek*, quite certain they were going to crash. But at the very last second, as the jump rose up in front of them, the palomino sprang up high into the air.

Champ chortled. *'Hang on, Livvy! This is how we do it!'*

Olivia felt her stomach lurch and for a moment, as they launched into the air, it was as if she was flying. And then Champ was landing nimbly on the other side and before she knew it the palomino was off and cantering once more.

'Are you okay up there, Livvy?' Champ asked her. *'We can stop if it's really too scary.'*

'No!' Olivia said. 'Don't stop, Champ. I'm not

scared at all! In fact, the butterflies in my tummy have utterly vanished and I'm having the most amazing fun. This is brilliant!'

'I knew you'd love it once you got over your nerves and into the swing of things!' Champ cried. 'What do you say, Livvy? Ready to go for gold?'

'Totally!' Olivia said. 'Let's do it, Champ!'

'Wheee!' Champ flicked his mane and set his sights. 'Water jump ahead, Livvy! Hang on tight!'

Over the water they flew with room to spare, and then there was a gate and a solid brick wall. At every fence Champ bounded and bounced, and Olivia found herself thrilling to his powerful strides. Before she knew it they had cleared every fence on the course except the treble.

'This is the last combination, Champ,' Olivia said.

'If we get through this, it's a clear round!'

'Oh, Livvy!' Champ chortled. 'Watch me kick up a clean pair of heels! One, two, three - wheeeee!'

As they cleared the final jump and dashed

past the finishing flag the crowd were on their feet
cheering like mad.

'A clear round! Hooray for the Great Palomino!'

'Oh, well done, Champ!' Olivia hugged him as
they came to a halt. 'We won!'

In the centre of the arena the winners' podium had already been erected and Lady Luella was waiting for them with an enormous golden cup.

'Well, this is unexpected, Olivia.' Lady Luella arched an imperious eyebrow as she passed her the trophy. And then Lady Luella softened her expression and smiled. 'But well deserved too. You and Champ jumped beautifully. I hope this prize can be put to good use?'

Olivia looked inside the cup and saw that it was filled to the brim with gold coins.

'Oh, it's enough to buy rugs for all the ponies!' she said. 'Thank you, Lady Luella!'

'Would you like to ride a victory lap?' Lady Luella said. 'It's traditional to canter past the grandstand and wave to the crowds.'

'What do you say, Champ?' Olivia asked.

'Ummm, I'd like to, Livvy,' Champ replied, 'except the thing is I'm feeling a bit peculiar ...'

'You do look strangely sparkly all of a sudden,' Olivia agreed.

It was true. The palomino pony was glowing from the inside like he was made from pure sunshine.

'How weird! I've gone all tingly!' Champ said. 'Too much exertion over the jumps maybe? Something I ate?'

'No, Champ,' Olivia said. 'I've seen this before. It's the witch's spell. It's unbinding.'

Champ whimpered. 'Oh, it's all tickly inside me! Oh me . . . oh my . . . oh . . . oh—'

And suddenly Champ wasn't talking any more. The only things coming out of his mouth were the sort of noises ponies usually make – which is to say snorts and nickers and whinnies.

'Hooray! The spell is broken!' It was Eliza. She came running across the arena at breakneck speed, looking very excited. 'Oh, Livvy, I was in the grandstand watching when Champ began to glow.

At first I thought it was the gold cup that was making everything shiny and then I realised what was going on! You did it!'

'*We* did it!' Olivia said. '*Two brave girls* together!'

There was a cheerful nicker from Champ who tossed his mane as if to say, *Two brave girls – plus one superstar palomino showjumper!*

'Yes, Champ,' Olivia said. 'You certainly were telling the truth – you are an amazing showjumper.'

'He really is,' Eliza replied, 'and he's every bit as beautiful as I remember now he's a real pony once more.'

'Isn't he, though?' Olivia agreed.

'Olivia!' A voice as crisp as crystal glass came from the podium and the girls looked up to see Lady Luella holding a red sash. 'This is for Champ,' she said, placing it round the pony's golden neck. 'You are still welcome do your victory lap on him if you like?'

And so Olivia and Champ did just that, Olivia standing up tall in her stirrups and waving to the crowd as she rode past the grandstands, and Champ snorting and whinnying with delight, thrilled to be a real-life pony again after two hundred years of being bound by the witch's spell.

'Phew! That was the most fun ever!' Olivia was pink-cheeked with excitement as she pulled Champ to a halt back at the podium. 'Where has your mum gone, Eliza?'

'Oh, she had to dash off!' Eliza said. 'Horace the Hunt Master tried to double his gold by betting on the duck races, only he got caught cheating. He was bribing one of the ducks! Anyway, the angry mob got back together and started chasing him and he began lobbing black puddings at them. It all turned very ugly and Mama had to get involved. She's still there now, I expect, which is a bit of a relief as she was just starting another conversation about me moving back to the manor.'

'Perhaps we should head home too then?' Olivia said. 'Champ has earned some hay, I think, and the other ponies will be waiting for him.'

'Excellent idea!' Eliza agreed. 'And on the way what say we stop by the rug shop? We have a trophy-sized swag of gold coins burning a hole in our pockets!'

Chapter Nine

Back at Pemberley Stables, autumn's chilly weather had put a bite of frost in the air. The ponies were huddled and shivering in their stalls when Olivia and Eliza skipped through the door with armfuls of snuggly woollen stable blankets for them all. There was much nickering with joy as Olivia rugged them up, and even more whinnies of excitement and delight when they saw that yet another pony had been brought back to life.

In his stable, dressed in a tartan wool rug that looked very smart, Champ pranced about the place, flicking his mane and swishing his tail.

Olivia giggled. 'You know, even now he's a real-life pony again, I get the feeling that Champ is still a bit of a show-off!'

'I think that's true for all our ponies,' Eliza agreed. 'Even once the witch's spell is gone, there's always a hint of their old enchantment about them. Bess can still be a bit naughty, Prince is prone to being greedy and Sparkle loves to roll in the fields and get mucky. So it's no surprise I suppose that Champ should be a bit flashy.'

'He *was* telling the truth, though, about being a superstar showjumper,' Olivia said. 'Weren't you, Pemberley Golden Boy?'

'We spent all the gold coins on the rugs,' Eliza said, 'but we still have the cup.'

'Very true,' Olivia said, 'and I think it should stay with Champ, right here in his stall.'

She went to place the trophy on the windowsill

where Champ could admire it.

'And now I'd better be heading home,' Olivia said. 'It's almost dinnertime and Mum will be wondering where I am.'

'You'll come back tomorrow, though, won't you?' Eliza asked hopefully.

'Of course I will!' Olivia smiled. 'We've got *four* ponies to care for now. And more spells to unbind if we're going to save them all.'

Olivia would have loved to give her friend a hug goodbye, but she knew it would be no use. When she tried to wrap her arms round Eliza they would have slipped through her ghostly form as if the girl were made of smoke. And so, with promises she would return, she gave the ponies a stroke on their muzzles and Eliza a cheerful wave before heading along the lane towards home.

'You've been gone all day!' Mrs Campbell said

when Olivia bounded in the front door. 'How was your bake sale?'

'Such fun!' Olivia said. 'We turned them into fortune cookies and they were a sell-out hit and there was a showjumping grand prix at the end.'

'I bet you enjoyed watching that!' Mrs Campbell said.

Olivia didn't reply; she was busy rustling about in her bag, where three brightly papered packages bound with red-and-white string had caught her eye.

'That's odd, I thought we'd sold them all,' Olivia mused.

She took a closer look. 'Oooh, and they've got names on them!' she exclaimed. 'There's one for you, Mum, and one for Ella and one for me!'

'What's that?' Ella had just stomped into the kitchen and snatched the cookie with her name on it from Olivia's hands. 'Did you write these?' she asked suspiciously.

'No,' Olivia replied truthfully, 'I really didn't. The Great Palomino did it.'

Ella snorted. 'Sounds like the name of a horse!'

Olivia gave a knowing smile as Mrs Campbell opened hers.

'It says, "The roast is burning",' she said. And as she spoke she noticed smoke coming out of the Aga. 'Oh no! Dinner!'

She hurried to open the oven door and remove the roast, which was now burned rather black and crispy. 'How on earth did the fortune-teller predict that?' she said. 'Oh well, it looks like it's takeaway pizza for dinner tonight.'

'Mine next!' said Ella. She opened her cookie and read out loud. '"Your little sister has a secret at Pemberley Stables. Your snooping may yet uncover it."'

Olivia felt her heart pounding. What if Ella found out her secret?

She was about to tell her mum everything, but Ella gave a shrug and screwed up the paper and threw it away. 'Stupid boring cookie! As if I care about your secrets down at the dumb old stables!'

Olivia heaved a sigh of relief and then, with trembling hands, she unwrapped her own cookie. She had been expecting a message from the Great Palomino, but instead she saw Eliza's delicate spidery handwriting.

Your good fortune, Livvy, is mine too. For I am fortunate to have a best friend as kind and true and wonderful as you.

Love, Eliza

Olivia felt her eyes well with tears as she thought about her best friend, trapped for two hundred years by the witch's curse. And at that moment Olivia walked away from her mother and her sister and made a silent vow.

I swear, Eliza, I won't give up until every pony in Spellbound Stables is unbound from their dark enchantment. And on that fateful day, when all the ponies are free at last, you'll be a real girl once more and not a ghost and we can be true best friends.

Wishes and Weddings

Olivia blinked in the darkness. 'Ooh, I'm blind as a bat! Where are the lights?' She flicked on the switch and gasped. 'Eliza? Where on earth is the pony? She's gone!'

The stall was completely empty ... except for a giant heap of muck that had been dumped right in the middle of the room on top of the straw.

Eliza groaned. 'She's not gone at all. You're looking straight at her!'

And then Olivia saw that the mud heap was wobbling a little. Not just wobbling, but kind of jiggling and then ... it spoke!

'Hello, babes!' the mud heap trilled.

'Eek!' Olivia shrieked. 'The mud just spoke to me!'

The mud heap began jiggling even harder at this and a cloud of dust rose up as it gave a tinkling laugh.

'Oh, babes! Me a mud 'eap? You must be joking! Whatever are you on about?' The mud heap moved closer to Olivia and out of the gloom of the stall and now she could see that it had legs! And eyes, and a muzzle!

'Livvy,' said Eliza with a sigh, 'this is Sparkle.'

'You mean underneath all that mud is a pony?' Olivia gasped.

'She never used to be like this,' Eliza said. 'I can remember her well.'

Olivia nodded. Of course Eliza would know what the pony had been like. They had once been her very own ponies – until the day she'd had a fateful fall from her beloved pony, Chessie. Heartbroken, her mother, Lady Luella, called upon the Pemberley Witch to put a curse on the ponies to punish them and they had been trapped in time.

'When Sparkle was a real-life pony she was brilliant white, well groomed and with a silken mane and lustrous tail that were the envy of all,' Eliza went on.

'Poor Sparkle!' Olivia said. 'The Pemberley Witch has turned her into a mud-caked mess!'

'Oooh, babes, don't worry.' Sparkle shook her dusty mane. 'You took Sparkle by surprise is all. Give me a quick minute to fix myself up a bit . . .'

The mud heap shambled off to the other side of the stall and dug about in the hay, and when she returned there was a tiara stuck sideways in her forelock and she had drawn all over her grubby muzzle with bright pink lipstick.

'There!' Sparkle said. 'Sparkle's all gorgey-porgey now! What do you reckon?'

'Uhhh, much better?' Olivia still couldn't quite believe her eyes.

'Come in, come in, and make yourself comfy!' Sparkle swished the muddy thicket that passed for her tail and gestured for Olivia and Eliza to join her.

'Sit down! Sit down!' Sparkle beckoned, and Olivia noticed now that the stall was more like a teenager's bedroom than a stable. There was a bed with a duvet with hearts and crowns all over it and the walls were smothered in pictures torn from magazines.

'This looks exactly like my sister Ella's bedroom!' Olivia said.

The posters on the wall all seemed to be of the

same blond-haired boy. In the photos he was often doing very dashing things like sailing a ship or sword fighting or horse riding.

'Who's that boy?' she asked.

Sparkle chortled. 'Livvy, Livvy, Livvy! You've been living under a rock, babes! You must know Prince Patrick!'

'I'm afraid I don't . . .' Olivia replied. 'But you seem to like him a lot!'

'Oh, everyone loves Patrick,' Eliza agreed. 'He's very popular. Handsome, charming – you know, the usual stuff.'

'He's a dashing prince!' Sparkle confirmed. 'And now he's getting married!'

'So there's going to be a royal wedding,' Eliza said. 'And who is the bride?'

'Why the princess-to-be is Lady Petronella!' Sparkle cried. 'It's been in all the papers! They're completely over the moon in love! It's going to be the most amazey-mazey wedding dazey! I simply cannot wait! I am all lovey-la-la! Ding-dong! Wedding bells! Huzzah!' ...

To be continued ...

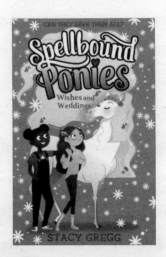

NEXT IN THE SERIES . . .

Rainbows and Ribbons

The very second the Spellbound pony's name was spoken, the stall began to fill with mystical mist. It rose through the straw on the floor in tendrils, going up and up until soon it filled the whole stall.

'I can't see a thing!' Olivia said.

'Me neither!' Eliza replied.

'You think you've got problems?' Another voice moaned through the fog. 'It's much worse for me. Enchanted mist plays havoc with my asthma, you know. Oh, and it feels all clammy against my fetlocks. Just my rotten luck.'

'The mist is clearing,' Olivia said. 'Oh, hello! There's a pony in here!'

The summoning had worked. Standing in the stall beside Olivia and Eliza was a very handsome pony with a wonderful, lush black mane and tail and a rich, russet-brown coat.

'Oooh. Hooray, he's a bay! My very favourite colour for a horse,' Olivia exclaimed.

'Humph!' The pony pulled a face. 'I doubt that very much. Now, if you had said your favourite colour was grey or even palomino, I might believe you. Those are stylish colours for a pony. Bay is boring. Just my rotten luck to be a bay, I say.'

'Er . . .' Olivia was taken aback. 'No, truly, it is my very fave colour! And it really is lovely to meet you. You must be Gus?'

'Yes. Not much of a name, is it?' The bay pony

sighed. **'Why, oh why couldn't they have named me something dashing like Prancer? Or a swashbuckling kind of name like Pegasus or Jet?'**

'Would you like me to call you Jet?' Olivia offered. 'I could, if that's what you want?'

'Oh, don't try and humour me!' Gus grizzled. **'It's far too late for that. I'm already in a very bad mood.'**

And to prove it, he did what ponies always do when they are moody and put his ears flat back against his head.

'Gosh!' Eliza pulled back in shock. 'He really is grumpy, isn't he?'

'He certainly is,' Olivia agreed. 'Eliza, I think we might just have found out what mischief the witch's spell has made this time. Poor Gus! It looks like he's been cursed to be grumpy.'

'Humph! Don't think you can just stand there and talk about me like I'm not even here,' Gus grouched.

'I can hear everything you say, you know. Which is typical. Just my rotten luck. Here I am, a talking pony, and no one even wants to speak to me.'

'Dear me.' Eliza shook her head. 'He really is very grumpy, isn't he? How do you go about un-grumping a pony?'

'We'll have to try to cheer him up somehow,' Olivia said. 'How about it, Gus? What would improve your mood? Do you like food?'

'Humph! What kind of food?' Gus grumbled.

'An ice cream perhaps?' Olivia suggested.

'Ick! No! Too cold on my tongue,' Gus griped.

'Fair enough,' Olivia said. 'Perhaps a slice of pizza, then?'

'It makes my hooves greasy holding the crust,' Gus sniffed.

'Lollies?' Eliza suggested, 'Or perhaps a sugar cube? Ponies always love sugar!'

'Oh, how can you even suggest such a thing?' Gus groaned, 'My poor teeth are aching at the very thought of it!'

'Right.' Olivia gritted her own teeth now, 'So food is off the menu. How about fun and games?'

'Oh, how I loathe fun!' Gus sighed, 'And games? Even worse!'

'No more fun and games, then,' Olivia said. 'Gotcha.'

'What else can we do?' Eliza wondered. 'There must be something that makes a pony happy.'

'Oooh! I know!' Olivia clapped her hands in delight, 'How about we go for a ride, Gus? Why don't I take you for a lovely hack?'

Gus sighed even more heavily. 'All right, then,' he said, 'but I won't like it.'

'That's the spirit!' Olivia said, putting on the biggest smile she could muster as she hastily grabbed Gus's saddle and bridle and threw them on before he could change his mind.

'Where shall we go, then?' she asked.

'Somewhere ghastly, I expect,' Gus said.

'I know just the place,' Eliza said.

But at that moment the stall began to fill with enchanted mist once more.

'Oh no,' Gus groaned, **'Here we go again! I'll be needing my inhaler if this keeps up . . .'**

When the mist cleared this time, they were in a very pretty forest. Dappled light filtered through the leaves of the trees on to an elegant lake where swans were gliding between bullrushes. The lake was bordered by wildflowers and running like a ribbon through the pretty scene was a bridle path.

'Oh, it's so beautiful!' Olivia gasped.

'Yes, and this bridle path winds all the way round the Pemberley lake,' Eliza said. 'I came here often with Chessie before I became a ghost.'

'It's all right, I suppose, if you like this sort of thing,' Gus sniffed. 'Although the wildflowers shall give me hay fever, I expect. Just my rotten luck.'

'All the same,' Olivia said, 'let's press on and try and make the best of it, shall we, Gus?'

She mounted up on to Gus's back. 'Off we go, then!' she clucked.

'Oww!' Gus squawked.

'What's wrong?' Olivia asked.

'I trod on a stone!' Gus grumped. 'Argh!'

'And what now?' Olivia asked.

'There's a gnat in my ear!' Gus said.

'There! It's gone. Better now?' Eliza asked.

'No. I can still hear buzzing,' Gus complained. 'Could be the honey bees on the wildflowers. They're so annoying with their smug *bzzz bzzz*. And the birds too! They're almost worse than the bees with their ridiculous tweeting. Why does all this ... nature ...

have to be here? Just my rotten luck!'

'I think we should give up and go home now,'
Olivia sighed.

'I think you're right,' Eliza agreed. 'He's hopeless.'

The girls put Gus back in his stall.

'Everything okay?' Olivia asked him.

'Hardly!' Gus whined, **'This hay is very dry, and the
water in my trough is very cold!'**

Olivia gave a heavy sigh. 'Right. Well I think we'll
be off home, then.'

'Livvy? Are you okay?' Eliza said.

'Not really,' Olivia replied. 'I was hoping I could
put Gus in a good mood but I think his bad mood has
worn me down. I've come over all gloomy myself.'

And Olivia trudged wearily out of the stable and
into the yard.

'Don't be sad,' Eliza implored her best friend as
she departed. 'Look, why don't you give Bess, Prince,

Sparkle and Champ a carrot before you go home?'

'All right, then,' Olivia sighed. But even as she fed the ponies their treats she couldn't shake her miserable mood and by the time she left for home she was feeling very glum indeed. Had they finally met a Spellbound pony that was impossible to save? . . .

To be continued . . .

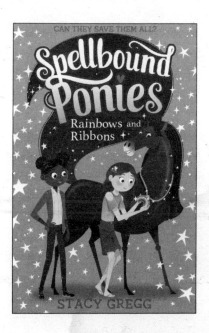

Out Now

them all!